The Twelve Trees Of Christmas

Teresa A. Barker

Independently Published

ISBN: 9798565079333

Credit given to Christopher P. Leach for the title of the book. Special thanks to Kate McGahan for giving me the inspiration to finish these stories that I started to write many years ago.

Here are the stories of twelve of the trees at The Christmas Tree Dump told in their own words. All had tales and secrets to tell of their very own Christmas experiences. Some happy, some sad, all quite different from each other. Some still dressed in their shiny gold and silver tinsel, some still adorned with the odd ornament that someone had forgotten or didn't bother to remove. There is every size, shape and shade of green that a Christmas tree could ever be, with the air filled with the glorious pine scent of the Christmas season.

Merry Christmas to all from the very special trees of the dump.

Contents

One

It can't be, it's too early, it's still Christmas! I guess that doesn't matter. This isn't how I was told it was going to be. It's not light yet; dawn is just breaking and here I am all alone at the Christmas Tree Dump. There are no other trees here.

"Please don't leave me here alone," I am screaming, but no one hears me. I was born to bring joy and happiness throughout the Christmas season. When I left my family at the farm I was filled with excitement and anticipation of what my Christmas would be like. I'd heard many tales from the grand elders of Christmases past, of how us trees make the world such a special place at this time of the year.

I wondered what would be in store for me as I was picked out and taken to my new home two days before Christmas. So many of my family and friends had gone to their new homes way before me. I was taken by a wealthy family consisting of a mother, father and two children. They seemed excited to pick me out and take me home. They all had a great time decorating me and trimming me with beautiful tinsel and such. The lights were hung on me like the finest jewelry. The most beautiful Angel was placed on my head.

On Christmas Eve night I was so excited to see all the presents displayed below my boughs. I could hardly wait for the morning. It came all too soon; there was a mad rush, the kids were up way before dawn. I watched as gift after gift was opened and set aside without hardly a glimpse of what was inside: the doll, the truck, the candy, everything I'd imagined and had been told about… but I had expected more. More excitement, more gratitude, more happiness. There were so many toys they could have made twenty kids happy, but for some reason not so for these two kids. I looked around and noticed they already had enough dolls and trucks for twenty kids. Still, this was Christmas and this was just the beginning; I still had all the caroling and other glorious things to experience.

I was wrong. It was time for the family to go for Christmas dinner at the parents' house and I was left alone.

"Oh well," I thought to myself, "they'll be home soon and then I'll see what Christmas is all about." I had heard all about that magic feeling and how I would be a big part of it.

It was not meant to be. The family (I didn't even know the parent's names; the kids were Sophie and Jason) returned late at night and went straight to bed. They were going to go skiing in the morning.

Little did I know I would be going before skiing.

I was stripped down as soon as the coffee pot was put on. First my Angel, then the lights, then my tinsel and decorations. I had been used as a place to put the gifts underneath for two ungrateful, spoiled, rich kids.

As we started the drive I could feel my needles starting to fall; they were the tears of a proud pine tree. There were no goodbyes or thank you's from my family; I was just packed up and thrown from the truck. I now understood what the sign that said Christmas Tree Dump meant. I was being dumped, thrown to the ground on a dark and lonely field.

I was the only tree there.

"Where are all the other trees? Please don't leave me here alone." I was crying but no one was listening. I heard the truck drive off and I was left alone in the dark. I thought of all the beautiful Christmas stories I had heard of Christmases past as my needles fell like rain.

"Please let some other trees join me," I prayed. Just then I heard the sound of a vehicle pulling up beside me. The door swung open and out was thrown the most beautiful Douglas Fir I had ever seen. There were still glimpses of tinsel glistening from her beautiful proud boughs. As quick as a wink the door slammed and the vehicle was gone.

We looked at each other and smiled. We may not have had the Christmases we had both hoped for but I had a feeling I was going to have a new friend. The dawn was breaking and things no longer felt so bleak.

Two

"Thank you Mr. Christmas Tree, you have given us the bestest Christmas Day anyone ever had," Lindsey said as her dad gently lay me beside the other trees at the site. Her mother took her hand and they all smiled as they got back into their car and waved as they drove off.

Hi, my name is Douglas. I have had the most wonderful Christmas! I went to my family a week or so before Christmas, the day of the big snowfall. Lindsey picked me. She liked the way I looked. Jim, her dad, thought I was very sturdy and Jill, her mother, thought I was perfect. When I arrived home they shook me off and took me into the warm house. I was given a nice big drink for my trunk, which I really enjoyed as I was very thirsty. When I was dry they started decorating me with very special homemade decorations that Jill and Lindsey had made just for me. Jim gently attached many, many lights to me, so many I thought I would light up the whole world! All the time they were singing choruses of Christmas carols. They were all so excited for the big day!

On Christmas Eve night I thought I would break with excitement. The house was filled with love and laughter. I had my family, as well as Jill and Jim's parents who had come from out of town. They all sat around me eagerly waiting for Jim to flip the switch on my lights, then they all burst into song – first very loud, the later quietly and soft. They ate all kinds of goodies. We were all so happy! Lindsey left some milk and cookies for Santa on the mantle beside me. I must have dozed off for a while for when I awoke, the milk and cookies were gone and I was surrounded by gifts and packages.

The grandparents were the first up in the morning; they were so excited arranging everything beneath me, being careful not to damage any of my branches. Lindsey then ran into the room, so excited, her eyes were like saucers when she opened the special doll with the specially made outfit that she had so hoped for. Everyone was so happy. This feeling lasted all through Christmas. When I started to dry out and my needles started to fall faster than Jill could clean them up, it was decided it was time to take me down. Everything was carefully removed and packed away. I was told many times how much I was loved and that I was the best Christmas tree they ever had. I was so happy and proud. Christmas was everything I had hoped it would be.

Three

ell little lad, what's your name?" asked an old grandfather tree.

"Oh, I'm Nicky."

"Well Nicky, how was your Christmas?"

I replied, "My Christmas was wonderful."

I was picked because I was small and didn't cost too much money. My family was a Mum, Dad and three children. We lived in a very small apartment. The children made and hung paper chains all around me to make me look very handsome. On Christmas Eve night everyone went off to church to celebrate the true meaning of Christmas, they later gathered around me to sing Christmas carols and the glow of the fire lit up the room. It was so beautiful; I hoped this night would last forever.

Mum and Dad stayed up very late. They just sat there staring at me saying how handsome I was and reminiscing about Christmases past. It was so peaceful. They said they may not have much money but that they have everything that's important for a merry Christmas.

The children got up very early Christmas morning to find a gift for each of them. The girls received dolls and the boy received a truck. They were all so happy and excited about what Santa had left for them. Mum and Dad exchanged a hug and a kiss.

The whole day was spent sitting around me. They all enjoyed a beautiful turkey dinner that was given to them from the church as Jim had recently lost his job and money was tight. The house was full of love and laughter and I felt so lucky and special to be able to be a part of such a beautiful Christmas.

Four

I must admit I feel a little bit jealous when I hear about some of the other trees' experiences with their Christmas families. I didn't have such a good time.

I was excited when I got chosen and taken home by the young couple. They had fun decorating me and I enjoyed listening to the stories of their previous Christmases. The problem was Willum the cat. It was wild. It tormented me every chance it got. I tried to be friends but he wasn't interested. He would dive at me from every direction. One time he even tipped me. I had to be tied to the wall so that I wouldn't fall. It really frightened me, as well as breaking a couple of my branches. I lost many needles as I was so stressed out. His parents didn't seem too bothered. He knocked off every decoration he could get; he even broke a few. I tried to make my needles sharp to dissuade him, but no luck. I was actually looking forward to leaving the house even though I didn't know what would happen to me. I was relieved when I was brought here to the Dump. I am now amongst friends.

I know most people appreciate the Christmas tree, the fact that each tree has given up its life for human's happiness. Even though it is just for a few weeks, most of us do this willingly, but there are some people who show us no respect, completely ignore us and abuse us. Please if you are going to have a tree in your home, please appreciate it and treat it kindly. Give us a drink every now and then so we don't dry out. We will lose way less needles. We have feelings; we feel everything, especially love. I didn't know love with my family but I'm hoping and have faith that after I am chipped I will go to some amazing people's homes. I know I will as a couple of my friends here have invited me to go with them. The birds and the wind have agreed to help.

Five

"What about getting a tree?" Anne said to her Mum.

"Oh, I don't know; I don't think we will have much of a Christmas this year," replied her Mum.

"Oh please Mum. You know how I love Christmas."

Her mother agreed to get a tree, so off they went to the tree farm where Anne took her time looking around until she saw me. Her mind was made up. I was going home with them.

I didn't know until we were home what Christmas was all about, but I soon caught on. Anne had been diagnosed with cancer earlier in the year and the treatments weren't looking very promising. She had decided if this was to be her last Christmas, she would like to spend it in a warm place. We live in Western Canada and she had only known cold, snowy Christmases. She decided to spend Christmas in Mexico but to celebrate an early Christmas with her family. They weren't pleased but they respected her decision.

I was treated so well, I was decorated so beautifully, every decoration had a memory attached to it.

The night before Christmas Eve, everyone was in bed when Anne came and sat beside me. She was such a beautiful young woman. She sat silently staring at me, no lights on in the room except for me. She smiled, then started to gently cry. She told me of her fears and how much her parents wanted her to be home for Christmas. She felt like she was being very selfish but, at the same time, to have a warm Christmas was always her dream and this could possibly be her last chance. She sat quietly beside me for hours. I could feel her every emotion. This was a very special time for me, so I tried to make it very special for her also by twinkling my lights just a little bit brighter.

On Christmas morning the family had a wonderful time opening presents and savouring every precious moment they had together, until Anne left for her trip in the early afternoon.

The family were all terribly upset after she left, but her brother Mick reminded them how much they all loved Christmas and loved Anne too. They hoped that this would not be Anne's last, that they must keep the faith, that miracles happen at Christmas and that Anne had personally picked the tree so they should enjoy the day as much as possible. He put on a CD of Christmas carols and started to sing. It didn't take long before the rest of the family joined in.

Anne returned home a couple of days after New Year's. She had had a great time, was beautifully tanned and was full of hope that her treatments would kick in and start to work.

She said, "I'm 23 years old and not ready to leave this life." She was so positive and determined! I have a feeling she will make it; she will be just fine and get to enjoy many more Christmases.

I was blessed to have been able to spend my Christmas with such a special family.

Six

I was one of the fortunate trees that grew up in the forest, along with my little friend here. All of us forest trees know that one day we may be cut down and taken away, usually for people to enjoy at Christmastime. Some trees actually hope for this, most of us don't. We hope to spend our lives with our tree families and watch the forest grow and flourish. Of course this doesn't always happen… as in my case.

I saw the couple with the children looking around at the trees, paying close attention to the very young ones. They asked the children to pick the one they would like to take home, which they did. Then they proceeded to look at the rest of us. They were intending to remove two trees.

We are all very protective of our young ones, so I purposely drew them close to me, making my scent as strong as I could with the hope that they would pick me. I wanted to be the one to go with little Oliver, so that he would at least have some family with him and I could watch over him. I was fearful they would just take Oliver and go to a tree farm for a bigger tree, but it worked. They decided on taking me, actually it was me that picked them. Us trees are more intelligent than people think we are. We think and we feel everything. I explained to Oliver that although he would be cut at his trunk, his roots would stay in the forest forever and that our bird friends that rest on us will visit and relay any messages to his tree family. This put his mind at rest and he became quite excited.

Neither one of us knew what to expect when we arrived at the house. Fortunately we were placed very close to each other, in adjoining rooms. I could see him in the reflection from the window. I was to be the tree for the adults and Oliver would be for the children. We were both decorated beautifully; the children had so much fun decorating their own tree. A train set was set up to surround Oliver. That first night was quite exhausting for us both. Oliver seemed to enjoy all the attention from the children. After the decorating was done I was basically ignored until the gifts were placed beneath me.

There was a lot of excitement with other family members and friends stopping by over the few days of Christmas and New Year's Eve. Then we were packed up and brought here. There wasn't any care shown for me or Oliver; we were just thrown into the truck, driven here and thrown out of the truck onto the ground. I tried my best to keep Oliver as safe as I could so that I would take the impact of the hard ground. We were both a bit battered. I tried to comfort him as best I could but at least we are now amongst friends and family, as a couple of the elder trees who we knew from the forest are here too.

My message to people taking trees from the forest, a tree farm or grocery store is to please treat your trees with respect. Treat them well, give them a drink every now and then and love them. In return we will make your Christmas season merry and bright. We will fill your home with the scent of the season and we will love you. If you see our needles falling, check on us. Are we thirsty? Are we stressed? Maybe we are excited. Maybe we are being tormented by a pet. Remember, we have been taken away from our families and have given our lives for you. Please take care of us. We also love this very special season and we are very willing to help you to have the merriest of Christmases.

Seven

I had a very interesting Christmas season. I was picked out by two ladies from Dr. Lee's dentist office. I was placed in the waiting room of the dental office and was decorated very nicely one evening by all the office staff. The weekends were a bit lonely but I didn't mind too much as I had very busy weekdays with many people coming in for their appointments. Most sat and admired me before going in to see Dr. Lee. I didn't know what was going on in there but I noticed most people were very nervous before they went in, but very relaxed and relieved when they came out, so I knew he was helping these people.

I enjoyed my stay there but at the end of the day on Christmas Eve, Brian(one of the assistants) said he would drop me off at the homeless camp close to where he lives, as the office would be closed until after the New Year.

At the camp we were met by a couple of men who were very happy to accept me as a gift. I was placed in an area where people could sit around me. I enjoyed hearing and feeling everyone's story, from the teenage girl who had lost her dad who then became a victim of assault by her mother's boyfriend, the young man who had been beaten and abused all of his life until he couldn't take it anymore, the old man who had turned to drink after the passing of his wife and ended up losing his home, as well as the older lady who said she just couldn't stand being inside and wouldn't go to a shelter as she didn't like rules. The older people looked out for the younger ones and the younger ones kept an eye on the elder people. They all looked out for each other. Everyone had a story to share. Most of the day and all of the evenings and nights I had people around me; it was beautiful. I was pretty close to the fire pit, so it looked and felt very cozy.

On Christmas Eve and Christmas Day evening a few of the people would sing Christmas carols. I found it to be very beautiful and extremely touching as these people all cared greatly about each other, just like a family.

I stayed there until one really cold night; the next day a city worker came and brought me here to the Dump. I am happy to now be amongst my fellow trees and to listen to their Christmas experiences.

Eight

Early one morning a truck drew up carrying a whole group of trees. They were from a local hotel. They had been purchased to be used as a fundraiser for local charities, with each charity decorating a tree. The best decorated tree, which would be voted on by the public, would receive a sizeable donation from the hotel.

When they arrived, all the trees were very tired, with lots of needles gone, some with branches missing. Joy, who was the winning tree, explained that they had all had an enjoyable but very busy Christmas. They had to all look their very best at all times as they had people around them all day every day, comparing tree to tree. Some of the trees enjoyed the competition, others just enjoyed each other's company as they all came from the same farm.

The best part was when groups of school children would come and sing Christmas songs and carols. In all the busyness there were a few mishaps and several near tippings, mostly by young people who had had a couple too many eggnogs, but luckily no tree was seriously hurt or damaged.

Joy, the winning tree, was decorated with many different kinds of angels in many colours, sizes and shapes. She looked magnificent. The charity used the donation to help local teens.

Nine

As it was just starting to get dark, a large flatbed truck arrived carrying two giant trees. They were so much bigger than any of the other trees at the dump. They were the trees that had stood proudly outside the city hall. They were both perfect in every way. They came as a gift to the city from a sister city far away. They had grown up together in a most prestigious forest known for its beautiful trees. They had been shipped with the greatest of care and placed either side of the entrance to the city hall. They were so tall that large ladders were needed to hang the decorations. Although they were dressed in the finest of lights, the ornamental decorations were only put on the top halves of the trees to prevent them from being stolen.

There was a big celebration on the night they were lit for the public. Many families attended. There was music and hot chocolate, everyone was in the Christmas spirit, but later that night it was silent except for an elderly man and his dog. They sat on a bench by the trees for hours. They would come to visit every night. Some nights others joined them. A couple of times some rowdy teenagers did some slight damage trying to climb the trees, but the trees were so big they could handle the abuse. They made their needles extra sharp, which quickly stopped the climbers in their tracks. The public loved how beautiful their city hall was at this time of the year; they lit up the whole area of the town.

The trees were so proud that they were the ones chosen, but they had not wanted to leave their families. They had seen other family members being cut down to be used as Christmas trees but they ultimately knew their roots would always remain at the forest and that they would always be able to communicate with them using their bird friends as well as the wind.

They felt a bit nervous as they were unloaded at the dump, because of their size. They didn't want to squash the other trees or intimidate them in any way. They needn't have worried, when trees are in this situation, on top of each other, it's like they are having a group hug. They were actually protecting the smaller trees from the rough elements.

They enjoyed getting to know the trees from this part of the country that they had only heard about and the other trees felt the same way.

Ten

I heard some of the trees whispering about the old man who comes by every night. Even though I am very shy and very small I had to speak up. He's with me; he's my Christmas Dad. The other trees stopped to listen to my story.

My Dad had been alone for the last three years since his beloved wife passed away. A neighbor had noticed him at the tree drop off last year. He would just stand and look at the trees, breathing in their most beautiful scent. The neighbor had asked why he goes there every night and what he enjoys at Christmastime. He explained that he and his wife both loved Christmas and looked forward to putting up and enjoying their tree every year. He said they would usually drive out to the edge of the woods and cut down a small tree, as they had a very small living room. They would decorate it, sing carols and read beside it, enjoying every moment, especially the beautiful scent that greeted them each time they entered the house. He also said when they eventually took the tree to be dropped off, they would just stand and breathe in the wonderful scent of the season. He no longer had a tree but he still enjoyed spending time with the trees and breathing in the smell, it brought back such beautiful memories of his dear wife.

The neighbor remembered this and this year she set out to find a small tree to surprise the old man and bring him some Christmas cheer. After a long search at the tree farm, she saw me and knew that I would be the perfect tree for him.

She took me home where her kids all helped to decorate me. I had the most beautiful Star on my head! I was so proud to be chosen for this special Christmas. I was delivered to my Dad by the lady and her children who were all carol singing at his door. He was so shocked and delighted when he realized I was sent for him. He was overwhelmed that his neighbor had remembered his story and that she would be so kind to do this for him.

He was very emotional as he welcomed me into the tiny house. He told me all about his wife and how he could feel her there with him. No tree could ever get more attention than I received. I made sure my scent was as strong as I could get it. I lost many needles because of excitement, but he didn't care, he loved me so much.

We were both very sad when it came time for me to leave, but he told me he would visit me every night until I was chipped... and he's kept his word. I would get very excited when I would see him coming.

When I finished my story, the other trees were so happy for me that while he was there all of us made our scent strong. We brightened up the whole neighborhood with the scent of the season! The wind even helped us by blowing the scent in the direction of his home. He would stand there admiring us, but especially me, and sing Stevie Wonder's song, one little Christmas tree could light up the world. He was singing that to me.

Eleven

I never got to go anywhere for Christmas. I was unsold at the grocery store. Me and a few others were brought here to the dump on Boxing Day. We were placed at the side in case anyone wanted to come and take us home. We were all very disappointed that we didn't fulfill our destiny as a Christmas tree to bring joy at this very special time of the year.

I was quite shocked and surprised when, after being here for a few days, the loveliest old gentleman came by. He looked around, then spotted me. After a quick discussion with his wife, I was loaded up into the truck and we headed home. I was a little bit battered with a couple of branches missing, but this didn't seem to bother them. I had no idea where I was going as Christmas had passed, but they seemed very kind so I wasn't worried at all. I felt they would take care of me.

It turned out I was to be part of celebrating a Ukrainian Christmas, which falls a little while after the Christian Christmas. I learned some of their traditions and I listened to many stories of Christmas past. The Ukrainian Christmas begins January 6th which is their Christmas Eve. This is very special to them with many traditions.

They told me their name for a Christmas tree is Yalynka which means a symbol of peace and friendship. They set their table with an extra place set for a family member that had died during the year. A candle was lit and placed in the window as an invitation for a homeless person or a stranger to join the family in celebrating the birth of Christ. The table was set with a small piece of straw in memory of Jesus in the manger.

The meal was meatless, consisting of twelve dishes; a round loaf was placed in the middle of the table with a candle on top. There was meaning to every part of the meal. The family all had to fast until Christmas Eve night. After dinner everyone sat around me and sang carols, then they all went to church just before midnight. They also attended church the next morning.

I stayed with my family for the entire Ukrainian Christmas, which lasted until January 19th. We were all sad to say our goodbyes, but I was very happy to have had such a wonderful experience with such a beautiful couple.

Twelve

I could feel the other trees staring at me as my Dad, David, and his friend gently laid me down at the side by the fence so that I wouldn't get squashed by other trees that might be piled on top of me. I know I must have looked a little worse for wear as I had had a different experience from the other trees.

I was lovingly picked out by David last Christmas. He was so excited! He had a friend with him who would transport me home in his truck. I was a bit nervous when I was first brought into the house as I was greeted by Lizzie the dog and Beany the cat. We soon became very good friends. I even let Beany sleep in my branches occasionally.

As soon as we got home, Dad put on the Christmas music and brought out his very special decorations. He told me the story behind each one as he gently placed them on my boughs. Some brought up very happy memories, some quite sad, but very meaningful for him. Every evening after work he would sit in his chair reading, stopping every now and then to admire me. Lizzie and Beany were usually lying beside him.

He was so happy, one day he came home from doing his Christmas shopping and he had purchased special decorations as gifts for the special people in his life. I watched as he carefully wrapped each one in the most beautiful paper bags.

He lived alone with no family living close by, but he had many friends stop to give him greetings. Everyone called him Mr. Christmas, he loved the season so much. I had the most wonderful Christmas and was not looking forward to leaving his home. I heard many of his friends saying, "When are you going to take the tree down?" He would answer "Whenever it tells me it's time."

I stayed up in his living room for a few months, lots of my needles were gone, my scent had gone and I was getting tired, so one day he said it was time for me to move outside. I didn't know what that meant but I knew it was what was best for me. He took me to his back garden where he gently laid me on the ground. He said he could still admire me and that now I could be a refuge for birds and other critters that needed shelter, as previous trees that lived here have done. I loved it, I had so many visitors, mostly birds and mice. Most had known the previous trees. I even met some of the trees that had come back as chippings. Dad always had brought bags of the chippings every year.

I saw the new young tree that was brought into the house just before the next Christmas. I admit I was a bit jealous, but I knew Dad loved me as much as I loved him and that we will be connected forever. I gave the new tree a wink and a smile as he passed me on his way into the house.

I noticed a lot of the trees here were nervous at the thought of going through the chipper so I used my experience to reassure them that it doesn't hurt at all and that they can end up wherever they want to go after they are chipped. They just have to ask a friendly bird to pick pieces of them up and take them back to their Christmas home, their tree farm, or wherever they choose to go. I know, I have gotten to know many of my elders by different birds dropping chippings of them, so I was never fearful or alone.

All trees are special and have stories to tell, even after they are chipped. We never die, we just change. We feel everything… so please be kind to every tree you meet. Merry Christmas.

Printed in Great Britain
by Amazon